Stat Man

by

Alan Durant

Illustrated by Brett Hudson

To my footballing hero, George Best,
for all the pleasure he gave to me
and so many, many others

First published in 2005 in Great Britain by
Barrington Stoke Ltd, 18 Walker Street, Edinburgh EH3 7LP
www.barringtonstoke.co.uk
This edition published 2007

Copyright © 2005 Alan Durant
Illustrations © Brett Hudson

The moral right of the author has been asserted in
accordance with the Copyright, Designs and
Patents Act 1988

ISBN 978-1-84299-543-3

Printed in Great Britain by Bell & Bain Ltd

Barrington Stoke gratefully acknowledges support from the
Scottish Arts Council towards the publication of the
fyi series

Scottish
Arts Council
LOTTERY FUNDED

Contents

Chapter 1
Meet Arnie

Ten facts about me

1. My real name is Arnold James Kean. (My friends and family call me Arnie.)

2. I was called Arnold after my mother's favourite film star, Arnold Schwarzenegger. He was in *Terminator I*, *Terminator 2* and *Terminator 3*. (I am glad she did not call me

Schwarzenegger because it is a very, *very* hard word to spell.)

3. I am 10 years, 8 months, 13 days, 7 hours, 4 minutes and 7 seconds old.

4. I am 1.5748 metres tall (with no shoes on).

5. I weigh 44.62 kilos (with no clothes on!).

6. I have brown hair and green eyes.

7. I love football.

8. I do not like jelly.

9. My favourite football team is Real Madrid.

10. My nickname is Stat Man.

People call me Stat Man, because I love stats – statistics, facts and figures. And, best of all, I love football stats.

I can tell you which country won the first ever World Cup and when (Uruguay, 1930).

I can tell you the maximum length of a football pitch (130 yards or 118.872 metres).

I know which player has scored the most goals for England (Bobby Charlton, 49).

I know the nickname of Forfar Athletic
(The Loons!).

I know what Plymouth Argyle's ground
is called (Home Park).

Some people do not think it is
important to know these things.
Sometimes, when I tell my mum one of my
football facts, she says, "Arnie, I don't think
I need to know that." Sometimes my big
sister Ellie says, "Arnie, do I look like I
care?"

My teacher, Mrs Moody-Brown, once said to me, "I wish you put as much effort into your work as you do into football facts."

She does not understand. This *is* my work. It is not just football facts. It is history, maths, geography, sport and lots more.

Knowing stuff about football has helped me to speak French too. I can say "Jules Rimet". Jules Rimet is the name of a famous Frenchman. He invented the World Cup. The Jules Rimet trophy is what the World Cup trophy used to be called. Brazil were allowed to keep it when they won it for the third time in 1970. They beat Italy 4-1. Pele scored one of the goals. He was the best player in the world ever (my dad says). His real name is ... much too hard to spell! (It is even harder than Schwarzenegger!)

As you can see, I know lots and lots of facts about football. If you could win football matches by knowing lots of stats then my team would always win. But that isn't how you win football matches. You win them by being good at football. That is my problem. I am very good at stats, but not very good at football.

That is why I will not be on the pitch when my team, Lime Green Rovers, plays in the Cup Final on Saturday. I will be on the sideline. Some people play striker, some play midfield, some play in defence. I am a substitute.

My manager, Bernie Norris, says substitute is a very important position. "You know what happened with Manchester United in the European Champions League Final," he said to me after we won the semi-final. (See number five in my top five sub stats at the end of this chapter.)

"But I never come on," I said.

"Ah, one day, Arnie, one day," Bernie said. "Your time will come."

But will it come on Saturday?

Arnold's Journal

My top five sub stats:

1. Keith Peacock was the first ever substitute to play in the English League when he came on for Charlton Athletic against Bolton in August 1965. Before that season, substitutes were not allowed.

2. David Fairclough, who played for Liverpool from 1975-1983, was nicknamed "Super Sub" because he came off the bench to score so often.

8

3. Ammoniaci came on as a sub for the Italian club Lazio in a Serie A game against Roma in 1979. He was sent off before he'd even touched the ball!

4. Laszlo Kiss is the only substitute to have scored a hat-trick in the World Cup Finals. He did it for Hungary against El Salvador in 1982, when he scored after 70, 74 and 77 minutes – the fastest hat-trick in World Cup history.

5. Manchester United beat Bayern Munich 2-1 to win the European Champions League Final in 1999. Their two goals were both scored by subs: Ole Gunnar Solskjaer and Teddy Sheringham.

Chapter 2
A Bit of History

"Some people believe football is a matter of life and death. I can assure you it is much, much more important than that." A man called Bill Shankly said that and I agree with him. Bill Shankly was the manager of Liverpool from November 1959 to July 1974. Some people think he was the greatest manager ever. He won the Championship three times, the FA Cup twice and the UEFA Cup once.

I told my manager, Bernie Norris, about Bill Shankly at our last training session. "Well, I haven't won anything," Bernie said. Then he smiled and added, "If Lime Green Rovers win on Saturday, I will take you all out for a burger. Then you'll think *I'm* the greatest manager ever, won't you?" And the whole team shouted, "Yes!"

The best managers always find out about their opponents before a match. I decided to help Bernie by finding out as much as I could about *our* opponents, Sheen Sports. I did it at school on the Internet when we were doing history with Mrs Moody-Brown.

(We were supposed to be doing research about Tudor England.) I typed in Sheen Sports on the search engine and a web address came up. Lime Green Rovers don't have a website, but Sheen Sports do. I visited it.

This is what I found out. Sheen Sports are second in their league. Here is their record:

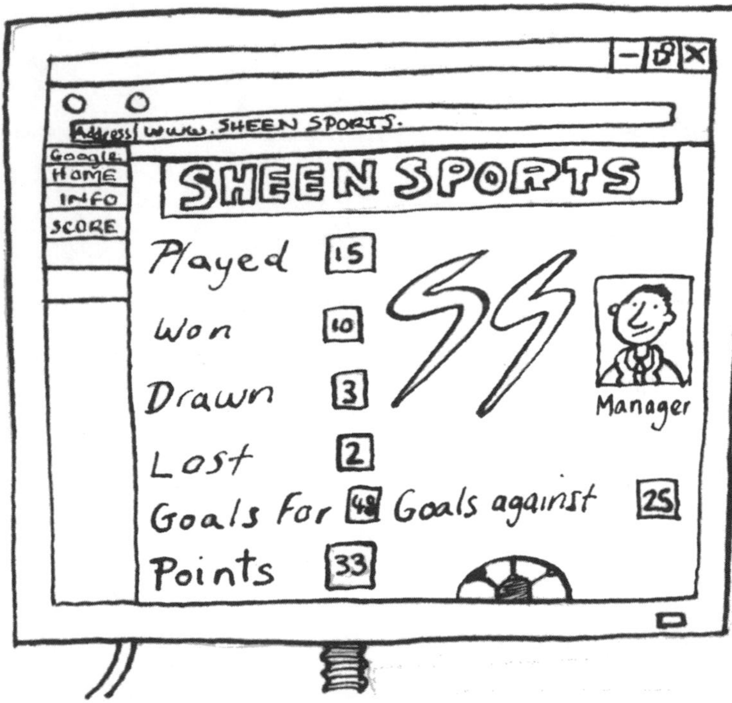

SHEEN SPORTS

Played [15]
Won [10]
Drawn [3]
Lost [2]
Goals For [48] Goals against [25]
Points [33]

Manager

Sheen Sports have a mascot. It is a bear called Besty. It belongs to the manager, Dave Potts. It was knitted for him by his mum.

Sheen Sports play in red shirts, white shorts and blue socks.

Their top goalscorer is Ben Shilton. He has scored 22 goals this season.

I was just looking at the Sheen Sports team photograph when Mrs Moody-Brown came to see what I was doing.

"Arnold," she said, looking at my computer screen. "That doesn't look like Tudor England. I know Henry VIII played tennis but I never heard of him playing football."

"He would have been very good in goal, Miss," I said. "He was so fat, no-one could have got the ball past him."

Mrs Moody-Brown laughed. "I wonder if the Tudors did play football," she said. "Perhaps you should do some research, Arnold, and find out."

"Yes, Miss," I said. So I did.

I found a website about Tudor games and sports. There was a whole bit about football. This is what it said:

"Football was a very popular sport in Tudor England. But it was very different then from the game we play today. Each side could have as many players as they liked. The goalposts were about one mile apart! Players could pick up and throw the ball as well as kick it into the opponents' net. The games were very rough and lots of people got hurt. A Tudor man wrote, 'Football is more a fight than a game. Sometimes players' necks are broken, sometimes their backs, sometimes their legs'."

I found out something else too – Henry VIII did play football! In 1526 he ordered a pair of leather football boots which cost four shillings! But he must have gone off football because in 1540 he banned it and said that anyone who played could be executed.

I told Mrs Moody-Brown what I had found out.

"That's very interesting, Arnold," she said.

I smiled because people do not often say that to me.

"Yes," I said. "It's history."

She asked me to read it out to the rest of the class. When I got to the end, Thomas

Jones put up his hand and said, "It sounds a bit like playground football, Miss."

"I hope it's not as rough as all that, Thomas," said Mrs Moody-Brown.

The bell rang for break.

"Now take it easy," said Mrs Moody-Brown. "Or *I'll* have to ban football too."

"Then if we play, you'll have to execute us," I said.

"Don't tempt me, Arnold, don't tempt me," said Mrs Moody-Brown. Then she sent us out to play.

Only four more days till Saturday!

My top five football history stats

1. In **1280** Henry de Ellington was killed playing camp ball (an early kind of football). He ran into a man on the other side wearing a knife in his belt and was stabbed in the guts.

 2. In the olden days, football matches were often played on Shrove Tuesday or pancake day – with a pig's bladder. Once, in Chester, they used the head of a dead Viking!

3. Lots of kings (apart from Henry VIII) banned football. In 1424 King James I of Scotland passed a law saying that 'na man play at the

Fute-ball". In the fourteenth century Edward III banned football because he wanted his subjects to spend more time doing archery. In the seventeenth century, Oliver Cromwell liked playing football when he was young. But he still banned it when he became ruler of England.

4. **On** Christmas Eve 1914, during the First World War, the German and British troops stopped fighting for a bit and played a game of football in no-man's-land between their trenches. (The Germans won 3-2)

5. In **1969**, when El Salvador beat Honduras to qualify for the World Cup, it started a war between the two countries that lasted four days. (So sometimes football really is a matter of life and death!)

Chapter 3
Training

It was training night, our last training session before the final. I put on my white Real Madrid shirt that my mum and dad gave me for my last birthday. On the back it has the number 7 and the name Raul. Lots of people say to me that I should have had the number 23 because David Beckham wears that. I like David Beckham, and Michael Owen and Zinedine Zidane and Ronaldo, but I like Raul best of all. He is the captain of Real Madrid and he scores lots of goals. He is also the top goal-scorer ever for Spain. His full name is Raul Gonzalez Blanco, but everyone calls him Raul. My mum thought I should have put Arnie on the back of my shirt, but I didn't think that Arnie sounded like the name of a Real Madrid player. In fact it didn't sound like the name of a footballer at all.

"I've never heard of any football player called Arnie," I said.

"What about Arnie Sidebottom?" my dad said.

"Arnie Sidebottom?" I said. I thought he was joking. Sidebottom sounded like a made-up name.

"Yes, Arnie Sidebottom," said Dad. "He played for Manchester United."

I still wasn't sure if Dad was joking, so I looked up Arnie Sidebottom on the web.

Dad wasn't joking. Arnold Sidebottom *was* a footballer. He was a centre back and played 20 times for Manchester United. He also played for Huddersfield. And he was a cricketer too. He played for Yorkshire and

he even played for England once in a Test Match against Australia. He scored two runs and took one wicket.
Arnie Sidebottom!

The whole team was at training – even Steven Morris. Steven Morris doesn't often come to training. He says he's too tired after school and needs a rest. That's what he tells Bernie anyway. He tells us that he doesn't need to train. He's good enough already. Someone told Bernie this last week and it made him mad.

He told Steven that he'd better be at training this week or he wouldn't be in the team for the final. So Steven came. I don't think Bernie would really have left him out though, because Steven Morris is our best player. He scored a hat-trick in the semi-final against Chalden Albion. He may be a big-head, but he can play football.

Steven Morris has an Arsenal shirt. On the back it has Henry 14. He says Thierry Henry is the best player in the world. He says Henry is much better than Raul. He says Raul is pants. He says I'm pants too, so it's right that I should have Raul on my back. He calls me Pants Man. I don't mind

being called Stat Man because I like stats, but I hate being called Pants Man.

"Hey, Pants Man," Steven Morris said when he saw me at training, "you'll have to get a new shirt soon, 'cos Michael Owen's going to take Raul's place in the Real Madrid team."

"No, he won't," I said. "Raul's the captain. He always plays."

"Not any more," Steven laughed. "He doesn't score enough goals – not like me."

He bunged a ball past our goalie, Fergus Boyle. Then he put his shirt over his head.

"Henry scores again!" he shouted.

"You should keep your shirt like that," called Fergus. "Then we won't have to see your big ugly head."

Bernie worked us hard at training. We did stretches and warm-ups and jogs and sprints. He had a new thing for us to do too. He put a kind of rope ladder flat on the ground and made us run along it, taking small steps so that our feet landed in the spaces between the rungs. I tripped over twice, but I wasn't the only one. Steven

Morris fell over twice too, but that's because he wasn't really trying.

"Steven! If you're not going to do this properly, I'll send you home."

"Sorry, Bernie," Steven said and he sounded like he meant it. I think he was scared that Bernie would chuck him out of the team for Saturday.

"Now let's do it one more time – and let's do it right," Bernie ordered.

I didn't fall over this time – but Steven did. He wasn't being stupid either. He really did trip over. Maybe he was trying too hard.

"Ow!" he moaned. He rolled about on the ground like he was in real pain. Everyone laughed because they thought he was fooling around.

"She fell over, she fell over!" Fergus chanted.

But Steven carried on rolling about and moaning.

"What's the matter, Steven?" Bernie said crossly. He didn't believe Steven was really hurt. But he was. He'd twisted his ankle. Bernie had to call Steven's mum to come and get him.

"Put some ice on that as soon as you get home," Bernie told Steven when he left, "and then strap it up with a bandage."

Steven nodded. His face was all white. For once, I actually felt sorry for him.

Bernie's face was pale with worry. He ended the training session early.

"Will Steven be OK for Saturday?" Fergus asked.

Bernie shrugged. "I don't know," he said. "But it doesn't look good." He turned to me. "Well, Arnie," he sighed, "it looks like you're going to be playing on Saturday."

He didn't sound very happy. He was looking at me a bit like I look at jelly (See number 8 of "Ten facts about me"). And I was all wobbly like jelly inside too. Me, Arnold James Kean, Stat Man, playing in the Cup Final. Who would believe it?

My top five Real Madrid stats

1. Real Madrid won the first ever European Cup (now called the European Champions League) in 1956 and have won it more times than any other team. They won it five times in a row from 1956 to 1960.

2. Alfredo di Stefano scored in all five finals. He is the record goal-scorer for Real Madrid with 307 goals. He also  scored more goals in the European Cup (49) than any other player. His nickname was the Blond Arrow.

3. In 1960 Real Madrid played in the greatest club game ever, beating Eintracht Frankfurt in the European Cup Final by 7-3. Alfredo di Stefano scored three goals and Ferenc Puskas, (nicknamed the Galloping Major) scored four. He is the only player ever to score four goals in a European Cup final.

4. Real Madrid have won La Liga (the Spanish Premier League) more times than any other team. The lowest they have ever finished is eleventh.

5. Two Real Madrid players, Zinedine Zidane and Ronaldo, have been voted World Player of the Year three times each.

Chapter 4
Cup Final Nerves

For a day I was very excited. Then I got scared. My mum couldn't understand it.

"You should be happy, Arnie," she said. "This is your big chance."

She was right, it was. But this wasn't how I wanted to get it. How could I possibly replace Steven Morris, Lime Green Rovers' best player and top goal-scorer? I knew I wasn't any good – that's why I was always sub and I never played. Just ten minutes or so at the end would have been fine for me, but now I was going to play the whole game right from the start. I was worried that I would let the team down.

On Friday I was so nervous I felt sick. I could hardly speak or eat.

"What's up, Stat Man?" Thomas Jones asked me at break.

I told him about the Cup Final.

"Wicked," he said.

I had to ask to go to the toilet twice during our history lesson. "Are you all right, Arnold?" Mrs Moody-Brown asked.

"He's just got Cup Final nerves, Miss," Thomas told her.

"Oh, why's that, Arnold?" said Mrs Moody-Brown – and I had to tell her about the Cup Final too.

"Well done, Arnold," she said. "I'm sure you'll do your best."

"Yes, Miss," I said. The problem was my best was nowhere near good enough.

At the end of the day as a treat, Mrs Moody-Brown said we could have a quiz. She split the class into teams and we had to answer questions. We were allowed to choose any subject we wanted. My team chose football.

We had to answer ten questions:

1. Which Scottish team plays at Fir Park?

(Motherwell)

2. What happened to the World Cup trophy before the 1966 finals?

(It was stolen. A dog called Pickles found it under a bush just before the Finals!)

3. Who scored a famous World Cup goal with the Hand of God?

(Diego Maradona in 1986 in a quarter final, his team, Argentina, beat England 2-1)

4. Which was the first British team to win the European Cup?

(Celtic in 1967, they beat Internazionale 2-1)

5. Who was nicknamed the Wizard of Dribble?

(Sir Stanley Matthews)

6. How wide must the goal be?

(7.3152 metres or 8 yards)

7. How high must the goal be?

(2.4384 metres or 8 feet)

8. Who is the only non-English team to win the FA Cup?

(Cardiff City in 1927)

9. What happened to Manchester City goalie Bert Trautmann in the 1956 FA Cup Final?

(He broke his neck! But his team still won 3-1 against Birmingham City.)

10. What was the longest penalty shoot-out in a professional match?

(44 penalties in November 1988 in Argentina. Argentinos Juniors beat Racing Club 20-19!)

The quiz was good because I got all the questions right and it stopped me thinking about the Cup Final for a little while. But the nerves came back as soon as it ended.

"Don't worry, Stat Man," said Thomas Jones. "It's normal to have butterflies before a final. Everyone does."

"Why does Arnie have butterflies?" asked Katie Lee. She didn't understand what we were talking about.

"He's got butterflies in his tummy," Thomas Jones explained.

"Yuk," said Katie. "Do you feel sick?" she asked me.

"Yes," I nodded.

"Arnie hasn't really got butterflies in his tummy, Katie," laughed Mrs Moody-Brown. "It's an expression. It means he is very nervous and he feels as if there are butterflies fluttering in his tummy."

"Oh, I see," said Katie.

"Now before we go home, I think we should all wish Arnie good luck for his match tomorrow," said Mrs Moody-Brown.

She counted to three and everyone shouted, "Good luck, Arnie!"

It was very nice of them and I know they did it to make me feel better, but it just made me feel more nervous than ever.

My dad tried to make me feel better too. "In the 1966 World Cup finals England's star striker Jimmy Greaves was injured," he told me. "Geoff Hurst came in to replace him and look what happened. In the final he scored a hat-trick and England won the cup!"

"I know," I said. "England beat Germany 4-2 after extra time. But I'm not Geoff Hurst. I'm not even a striker."

"Cometh the hour, cometh the man," said my dad.

I nodded, but I didn't really know what he was on about.

I waited all evening for Bernie to call and tell me that Steven was better, but he didn't. There was no escape. I was going to have to play.

My top five striker stats

1. Pele scored 1281 goals in his career playing for Santos, Brazil and the New York Cosmos.

2. In a World Cup qualifying match in 2001, Australia beat American Samoa 31-0. Archie Thompson scored 13 goals, a record for an international match.

3. Kenny Dalglish is the only player to score 100 league goals in both Scotland and England.

4. "Dixie" Deans of Everton holds the record for the most goals scored in an English league season with **60** goals in 1927-8.

5. Geoff Hurst is the only player to have scored a hat-trick in a World Cup Final.

Chapter 5
Nightmare

It was awful. I could not find my boots. I searched everywhere but they had gone. I had to play in my socks. We were losing 1-0. The ref awarded us a penalty in the very last minute. He said I had to take it.

"But I can't," I said. "I've got no boots."

"You must take it," he said.

I put the ball on the spot, but it kept moving. The ref blew his whistle. I ran up to the ball. It moved. I kicked and thump! I fell over on my bottom.

"Ow!" I woke up on the floor with my duvet on top of me. I was sweating all over and shaking like a jelly. I could not move for a second or two. Then I sat up and sighed. It had just been a nightmare. Thank goodness! Then I remembered what day it was and I started to sweat and shake all over again!

I couldn't eat breakfast. The butterflies were fluttering in my tummy again and I felt sick. I got my kit together. A sock was missing.

"Mum, I can't play!" I shouted. "I've only got one sock. Quick, phone Bernie and tell him!"

My mum just laughed. "Your sock is right there on the floor in front of you, Arnie," she said. She was right.

"Don't worry, Arnie, you'll be fine," my dad said when we got to the football ground. I was too nervous to reply. I got out of the car and walked over to the changing rooms.

"Good luck, Arnie!" my mum called. *I'm going to need it*, I thought to myself.

The changing room was very noisy. Everyone was very excited. Fergus came over and thumped me on the back.

"Way to go, Stat Man," he said. "Hope you've got your shooting boots with you."

I smiled weakly.

"Cheer up, Arnie, it's the Cup Final not a funeral," said Bernie. But he didn't look that happy himself. I knew he was wishing Steven Morris was fit to play. I was sure the whole team were – and I didn't blame them. I was wishing it too.

When we were all in our kit, Bernie called us round for a last team talk.

"Now, boys," he began, "Sheen Sports are a good team as we know from what Arnie found out."

"What, that their mascot is a bear called Besty?" said Fergus with a grin.

"It's their players I'm talking about, not their mascot," said Bernie. "This is going to be a tough match. Now ..." He got no further because the door crashed open and Steven Morris walked in.

"Ta-da!" he shouted. "The star returns. I'm fit and ready to score." For a moment everyone stared at him as if they were in shock. Then they all cheered – well, all except Fergus and Bernie and me. I thought Bernie would be smiling now but he wasn't.

"Steven, I thought your ankle was still too bad to play," he said. "That's what you told me last night."

"Yeah, well, this morning it's better," said Steven.

Bernie frowned. "Then why didn't you tell me earlier?" he said.

"I thought it would be a nice surprise," said Steven.

"It is," said Bernie. "But I've told Arnie he can play now, so you'll have to start as sub."

There was a gasp of shock from everyone – even me this time. How could Bernie play me instead of Steven? And that's exactly what Steven thought.

"You can't play Pants Man instead of me," he said.

"It's only fair," Bernie said. "Arnie deserves his chance." He gave me a warm smile that made me feel good inside. But I knew what I had to do.

"It's OK, Bernie," I said. "Let Steven play. We've got a much better chance of winning the cup with him in the team. I'll be sub." I gave a small smile. "It's my position after all." And that was it. I'd given up my chance to play in the Cup Final for big-head Steven Morris. I was sad for a moment, but then all I felt was relief. At last, the butterflies had stopped fluttering.

Arnold's Journal

My top five mascot stats

1. In May **2002**
Hartlepool's mascot,
H'Angus the monkey, was
elected the town's mayor!

2. At half-time in a game between
Swansea City and Millwall, Swansea's
mascot, Cyril the Swan, ripped the
head off Millwall's mascot, Zampa the
Lion, and kicked it into the crowd.

 3. The World Cup Finals
always have a mascot. The
strangest one was for the
Finals in Spain in **1982**. It
was an orange, with arms
and legs, called Naranjito.

4. Every year since **1999** there has been a British **M**ascot **G**rand **N**ational race. **T**op mascot so far is **O**ldham **A**thletic's **C**haddy the **O**wl, who has won twice.

5. David Beckham's first appearance on the pitch for Manchester United was not as a player, but as a child mascot, in the game against West Ham in **1987**.

Chapter 6
The Final

I joined in the warm-up and then went to the touch-line when the game was about to start. Bernie handed me a pen, a piece of paper and a stop-watch on a string.

"Arnie," he said, "I know how you love your facts and figures. I thought you might like to keep the match stats for the final."

I grinned. "Thanks," I said. So I was going to play an important part in the final after all!

I put the stop-watch round my neck. Then I drew a line down the middle of the paper. On one side I wrote Lime Green Rovers and on the other side Sheen Sports. Then down the left edge of the paper I wrote: Shots on Target, Shots off Target, Goals, Corners, Fouls, Yellow Cards, Red Cards, Subs, Final Score.

The first half was very even. Both teams played hard. I put a lot of ticks next to Shots off Target, Corners and Fouls, but none next to Goals. At half-time it was nil-nil. I chatted to my mum and dad on the touch-line and told them what had happened, while Bernie gave his team-talk.

"What a shame you aren't playing," said Mum.

"It's OK, Mum, because I'm keeping all the match stats," I said and I showed her my piece of paper.

"It's good to see you're taking part in some way," said Dad.

I was very busy in the second half. I had a lot more ticks to put next to Shots on Target. Most of them were on the Sheen Sports side of the paper. Fergus had to make three great saves to stop them from scoring. At the other end the Sheen Sports goalie made a good save too to keep out a shot by Steven Morris

At last I put a tick next to Goals – but the bad thing was it was for Sheen Sports. It was scored by their top scorer, Ben Shilton, after 12 minutes and 43 seconds of the second half. The Sheen fans shouted and hugged each other. The Sheen manager, Dave Potts, waved his bear Besty in the air.

"Come on, boys!" he called.

"Let's have some fight, Lime!" Bernie shouted.

In the next ten minutes I put three ticks next to Corners, four next to Shots off Target and two next to Shots on Target for Lime Green Rovers. I was so nervous I chewed the end off Bernie's pen!

Then Fergus kicked the ball upfield. Steven chased it. He went past one defender, and another. The goalie came out. Steven shot. The goalie touched the ball but could not stop it ...

"Goal!"

I jumped in the air. So did Bernie. He banged me on the back.

"We're back in it!" he said with a laugh. His face was one big grin. But the grin soon became a frown.

Steven Morris was lying on the ground with his shirt over his head. At first everyone thought he was just celebrating his goal, but then he started rolling around and groaning. He'd tripped over and hurt his ankle again!

Bernie ran on with some water. He put it on Steven's ankle. Then he helped Steven up. But Steven couldn't walk. "Ow!" he yelled every time he tried to take a step. Bernie had to carry him off.

I watched and then suddenly my tummy started to flutter again. I was going to have to play!

"You're on, Arnie," Bernie said. "Good luck. Go up front and just do your best." His face looked grim now.

"But who's going to keep the stats?" I asked.

"It doesn't matter, Arnie," Bernie said. But he took the paper and pen from me.

"Are you coming on, son?" the ref said. "We haven't got all day."

He was right there. There were only 2 minutes and 12 seconds of the match left.

"You'd better give me the stop-watch too, Arnie," said Bernie. So I did.

Then I ran onto the pitch. My legs felt as heavy as huge rocks. The butterflies were back too in my tummy.

"Go, Arnie!" my dad shouted.

I waved and then ran to the centre circle for the kick-off.

For the next two minutes I ran around as if in a dream. I didn't touch the ball once. Lime Green Rovers got a corner. Everyone but Fergus was in the Sheen Sports half.

I stood on the edge of the Sheen six yard box and waited for the corner kick. I suddenly thought about my stats page and turned to see if Bernie had remembered to put a tick next to Corner.

The next thing I knew someone shouted my name and I started to turn round again when ... thump! Something banged against my head and knocked me over. I lay on the ground for a moment, not sure what was going on. Then there was another shout, really loud this time, and someone fell on top of me and hugged me! I thought I must be having a strange dream. I shut my eyes and opened them again. No, I was awake.

A hand reached down and helped pull me up. A face grinned at me. It was Fergus.

"You did it, Arnie, you did it!" He put his hand up for a high five.

"Did what?" I asked.

"You scored!" said Fergus. "You've won us the cup!"

I looked over at the Sheen Sports' goal. The ball *was* in the net. I'd scored. I'D SCORED! It may have been the luckiest goal in history but it didn't matter. I'd scored the winning goal in the Cup Final!

There wasn't even time left to take the kick off. The ref blew his whistle for the end of the match. Lime Green Rovers had beaten Sheen Sports by 2-1.

"Well done, Arnie!" my mum shouted.

"Great goal, son!" my dad shouted.

"Hey, super sub," said Bernie and he shook my hand. "That was like Manchester United against Bayern Munich in the Champions League Final."

He handed me the sheet of stats. "You should keep this," he said.

I looked at the sheet. He had marked up the corner. The only thing he hadn't noted was my goal! He must have been too excited.

Later, back home, I made up a proper stat sheet and stuck it on my bedroom wall.

This is how it looked:

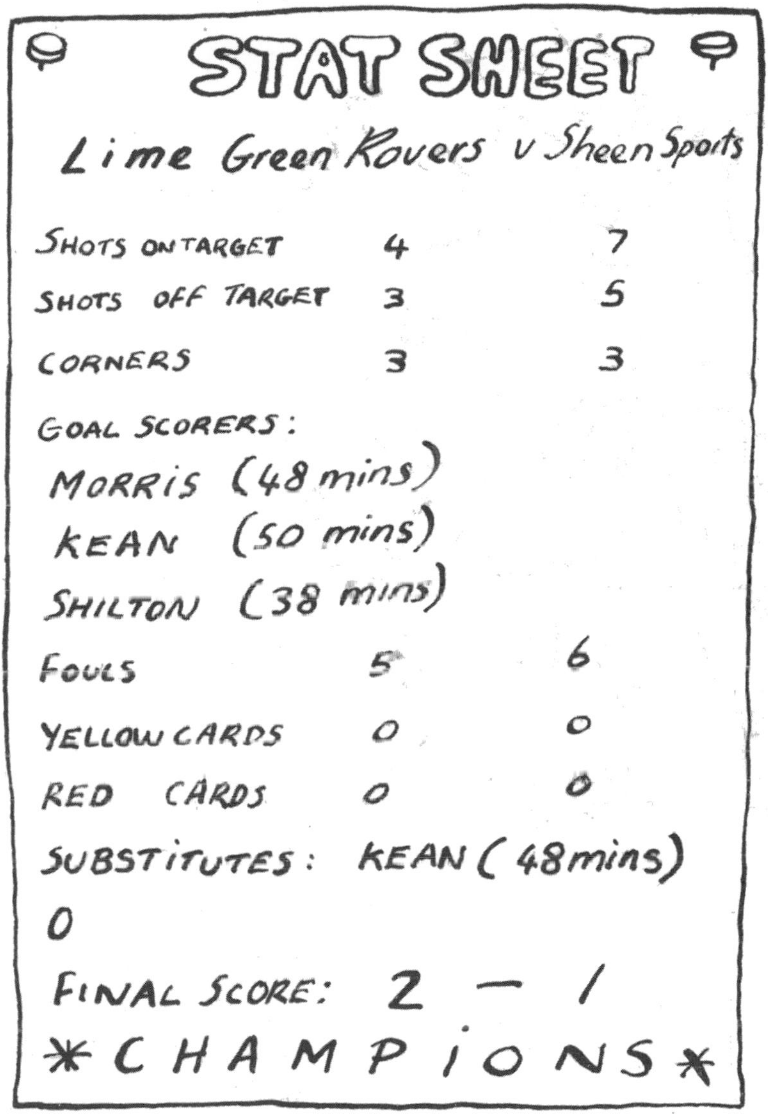

STAT SHEET

Lime Green Rovers v Sheen Sports

SHOTS ON TARGET	4	7
SHOTS OFF TARGET	3	5
CORNERS	3	3

GOAL SCORERS:
MORRIS (48 mins)
KEAN (50 mins)
SHILTON (38 mins)

FOULS	5	6
YELLOW CARDS	0	0
RED CARDS	0	0

SUBSTITUTES: KEAN (48 mins)
0

FINAL SCORE: 2 — 1
CHAMPIONS

Every night I look at that stat sheet and grin. I remember the day that I, Arnold James Kean – alias Arnie, Stat Man, Pants Man, Super Sub – scored the winning goal for Lime Green Rovers in the Cup Final. And that's the best football stat ever!

My top five Cup Final stats

1. J. F. Mitchell is the only player to have worn glasses in an English FA Cup Final. He was the Preston goalie in 1922 when they lost 1-0 to Huddersfield.

2. In the first ever Scottish Cup Final in 1874 Clydesdale striker James Long, kicked the ball into the Queen's Park goal. But there were no goal nets and the ball bounced back into play off a spectator's knee. The ref didn't give the goal and Queens Park won 2-0.

3. Jimmy Delaney won Cup medals in three different British countries: in Scotland with Celtic (1937), in England with Manchester United (1948) and in Northern Ireland with Derry City (1954).

4. Denmark didn't qualify for the Finals of the European Championship in Sweden in 1992. They finished second in their group to Yugoslavia. But Yugoslavia was not allowed to play, so Denmark took their place and went on to beat Germany 2-0.

5. Only one World Cup Final has been won on a penalty shoot out: Brazil beat Italy 3-2 in 1994 (the match score was 0-0). Italy's best player Roberto Baggio missed the final penalty.

THE
END
A
r
n
i
e

AUTHOR FACT FILE
ALAN DURANT

Which football team do you support?

Manchester United

Who is your favourite ever player?

George Best (and my son Kit!)

What was the first match you ever saw?

Fulham v Burnley (Saturday 10th February 1968. Fulham won 4-3)

What was the best match you ever saw?

Fulham v Manchester United (Saturday 5th October 1974. Manchester United won 2-1. The crowd size was ... I'm not that sad!)

Do you think England will ever win the World Cup again?!

Yes, and pigs can fly.

ILLUSTRATOR FACT FILE
BRETT HUDSON

Which football team do you support?

Liverpool when I was younger

Who is your favourite ever player?

Thierry Henry

What was the first match you ever saw?

Liverpool v Wimbledon

What was the best match you ever saw?

Euro 96: England v Germany

Do you think England will ever win the World Cup again?!

Yes!

Barrington Stoke would like to thank all its readers for commenting on the manuscript before publication and in particular:

Michael Amos	Rebecca Gault	Mrs Nash
Josh Anderson	Luke Hall	Joseph O'Riordan
Qasim Azair	Peter Hanson	Savvas Paphitis
Grant Brown	Karenprit Hear	Brendan Pollitt
Ryan Buchanan	Harres Khan	Sarah Raeburn
Sue Byrne	Fiona Lyall	Amy Roberts
Malika Chopra	Liam Lyall	Gabriella Rose
Blake Daniel-Ryan	Elise Malcolm	Jack Smith
James Dewsnap	Jody McGhee	Holly Smith
Nicholas Doran	Ryan McNaught	Paul Somerville
Chloe Edmond	Harriet McPheely	Jason Sweeney
Antony Faver	George Meredith	Helen Taylor
Linzi Ferrier	Craig Millar	Krishan Unadkat
Fraser Flett	Leah Mitchell	Connor Urquhart
Natasha Foale	Ben Mottram	Kieran Woolley
Keir Gardiner	Joe Mottram	Mackenzie Wright

Become a Consultant!

Would you like to give us feedback on our titles before they are published?
Contact us at the email address below – we'd love to hear from you!

info@barringtonstoke.co.uk   www.barringtonstoke.co.uk

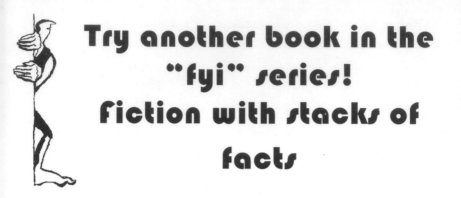

Try another book in the "fyi" series!
Fiction with stacks of facts

The Environment:
Connor's Eco Den by Pippa Goodhart
The Internet:
The Doomsday Virus by Steve Barlow and Steve Skidmore
Scottish History:
Traitor's Gate by Catherine MacPhail
Space:
Space Ace by Eric Brown
Vikings:
The Last Viking by Terry Deary

All available from our website:
www.barringtonstoke.co.uk